DADDY'S SECURITY

A Dark DDlg Ageplay Instalove Erotic Romance

Sonia Lake

CONTENTS

CHAPTER ONE

Elle

Warm sunlight spills over the highly polished marble floor. My slippers pad quietly down the hallway toward the kitchen as I rub the sleep from my eyes. A big yawn spreads over my face as I open the fridge and pull out my fruit and veggie smoothie. Melinda, my chef, prepares one every day by six. The morning is the only part of the day that I have to myself.

The golden light shines off of the sleek floor to ceiling windows that look out over the Hollywood Hills. My stylish, hollow, lavish cage. With a heavy sigh I lean my body against the door and step out onto the deck.

There's a slight chill in the morning air that casts gooseflesh over my skin. Leaves rustle and shimmer in the breeze as I scan the rolling landscape. The thick, gritty liquid slides down my throat and I swallow hard. Bless Melinda. It's as tasty as it possibly could be.

Between the beauticians and the dietitians, the estheticians and the hair technicians and the Eastern physicians, I scarcely have a moment alone to savor the bitter taste of my own loneliness. Most of the time I'm a canvas — blank and vacant until I'm altered by someone with a vision.

Sometimes it's a style crew dolling me up for social media to sell supplements I don't take and tea I don't drink. Sometimes it's a director, cuing me as I emote passion and longing into the empty face of some generic, chiseled hunk. I've played women falling in love over and over, but I've never known love myself.

Cal, my first manager, came into my life at 19. He was a friend of my parents. My mother, a vapid, aging starlet whose carved and sculpted face is a mask of constant, vacant surprise. And my father, the erratic, "genius" director, who's more fond of old scotch and young interns than he ever was about our home life.

Lets just say it was easy for Cal to bend me to his will. I was so starved for attention that I couldn't differentiate between romance and his obsessive control. He sensed the scared, lonely girl inside me and dug his claws in deep.

Over time he pruned me to his liking — I lopped off any part of myself that didn't please him. He told me how to dress, how to speak, how to fuck. When he insulted my appearance, he told me it was for my own good. He pointed out my faults to make me stronger, he'd lie. Knots twisted in my stomach and throat all the time, but I didn't know any other way.

By no choice of my own, I became his possession. My spirit wilted. My body wasted away from the stress and near-starvation diet. After a few years, I noticed the change, but I discounted my observations. It took me seven years, countless breakups, and a private security force to finally end our relationship.

I'm twenty seven, as of last week. Practically geriatric in Hollywood years. I scowl as I gulp down the dregs of my smoothie, cursing for the millionth time this epic testament to greed, consumption, and superficiality.

Enough, Elle. Forget all that and smile.

My mother's favorite advice rings in my ears as I step back inside. The faux-fur edge of my peignoir tickles against my calves as I walk over to the sink. To my left, toward the entrance and foyer, stands a muscular man in black pants and a black t-shirt. In small, grey text on the chest, the shirt reads "McCarten Security."

Yeah, about that. Cal didn't exactly fade into the background when I left him. Every time I'd try to take off, he'd reel me back in, doting on me and pampering me for a time. Then the cruelty and control would come back tenfold. This last time, I only made it because I'd taken months to move money, contact attorneys, and find my own home.

Then the emails started. Long, horrifying diatribes about my worthlessness and inevitable demise. Furious, coke-fueled voicemails. It was an Olympian effort to keep one step ahead of him.

Somehow, he found my address. I started getting a mix of gifts and garbage in the mail. Then, last month, he shattered a window and broke in. Thank god I'd installed an extensive alarm system. I pushed my shelves up against my bedroom door, pulled the revolver from it's lock box under my bed, and shook as he beat against the door and screamed at me.

I'd called McCarten's that night. Nickle, an old co-star and friend, recommended them. You don't get a name like Nickle unless your parents are sure you'll never have to work for one in your life. Her parents are both actors — happily married, somehow. She's kind, and sweet, but not especially interesting. Still, I appreciate having someone who, to some extent, understands my situation.

"Good morning," I call toward the man in the foyer. He straightens his posture and gives me a curt nod.

Hmph. Here I am in my baby pink dressing gown, silk teddy, and matching faux-fur slippers and he doesn't even bat an eye. Can't even bother to sneak a glance as I turn around.

Am I desperate? Absolutely. Is it pathological to expect any man I choose to bend to my will simply because it's what I want? Probably, yes. And I don't need him reminding me of those things. The company will have to send someone else over. Someone squat and ugly, I hope.

This stoic sentry has gotta go.

I flip open my personal phone and pull up McCarten's number. My staff handles my entire online presence, and after the ordeal with Cal, the simplicity makes me feel secure. Anything I have to do online, I do on my computer, which I've had secured and re-secured by IT experts.

A gruff voice answers after two rings. "McCarten's Security, this is Leroy speaking."

Leroy. I'd have remembered that deep voice. It was a polite, cheerful woman who'd help me set up services with them.

"Hi, this is Elle Hawthorne," I say in my silky, easy actress voice.

"Mhmm," he grunts. As if he doesn't even know what that means. I bristle and continue, unable to keep the sour note from my voice.

"Anyway, I'm gonna need to have a different guard at my house," I tell him declaratively.

"Have my men been unsatisfactory? Or unprofessional?"

Hmph...shit. Not really. My tongue catches in my throat for a moment. For an actress, I'm an unnatural liar. It makes me uneasy.

"I, um, want someone more...attentive," I manage.

He pauses for a moment. In the quiet I can hear muffled keyboard clicks. As I open my mouth to speak, he responds.

"I understand, miss. I got your file right here. I'll see to your needs personally tomorrow."

"Thank you, I—" A beep cuts me off.

He hung up. He hung up?! Who the fuck does business like that? Whatever. Guess I'll have the pleasure of meeting that jerk tomorrow in person.

My staff start rolling in around 9 AM. Today, we're shooting bathing suits by the pool, vitamins in the kitchen, makeup, and hair extensions. They'll sprinkle that content in throughout the week with their "organic" content — staged, made-up, digitally altered photos of me "living my life." Yuck.

A more honest portrait would be me, bare-faced with twin braids running down my back as I play with blocks and puzzles in my room. Maybe I should endorse the shop that sells the adorable onesie pajamas I love so much. That'd be the day, I chuckle bitterly.

No, that's a secret that's just for me. I don't know how I'd explain it to someone else. It lets me experience things I don't think I felt as a child — curiosity, playfulness, hope, joy.

Innocence. It gives me a glimpse of innocence. A brief reprieve from my critical mind that never stops churning. Regression helped me cope once I was finally free from Cal.

The allure of little space makes me listless throughout the rest of the day. I move through it, smiling when I should, only a quarter present. The rest of me is dormant, tucked far away.

There's a beautiful sunset tonight. Rosy pink and tangerine hues reflect in the calm surface of my pool. A crimson sun shines through the cloud cover. For some reason, the beauty makes me ache.

CHAPTER TWO

Leroy

I furrow my brow as I enter Elle's address in my GPS. We haven't met, but she's already a pain in my ass. She called yesterday to find a replacement for Richard — my experienced, cool-headed second in command. Known for being rock solid, reliable, and quiet. He's been with the company nearly as long as me, and I started the damn thing.

He knows when to keep his fucking head down. I have a suspicion that's the problem Elle couldn't quite articulate over the phone.

Minimalistic, open, modern mansions blur by as I wind up through the hills to her address. Jesus, there must be a factory somewhere that cranks these things out. All clean lines and glass. Beautiful, in a tasteless, overpriced sort of way.

I'm afraid the woman I'm meeting today may be the same way. I've dealt with more than a few desperate cougars who've confused my security company with a rent-a-dick business. From the amount of propositions I've gotten, I think it'd do quite well.

It always goes the same way — they're sweet and flirtatious when I arrive. When I turn them down, they fire the company. Anything for a little morsel of power.

Guess that's what happens when generational wealth insulates you from ever having to meet a challenge. These types are spoiled from the cradle to the grave.

Elle needs discipline. Good that I know a thing or two about getting brats in line. But that's off the clock. And definitely not with rail-thin movie stars.

I pull into the driveway and look the house over. There's a line of vehicles edging the circular drive — her staff, I'm guessing. They're well-worn sedans and hatchbacks, not the sleek status symbols I've seen on display at so many work sites.

As I approach the door, a short, curvy woman in a black button down and chic houndstooth pants leads me inside. I may not look like a man who cares for style in my black pants and work shirt, but I can appreciate a well-chosen outfit.

I think about complimenting her but decide against it. Women like Elle will use any bit of ammunition they can find to stir up trouble. I won't be giving her any.

"Miss Hawthorne will be right down. Can I get you anything? We have coffee, tea, kombucha…" she trails off when I lift my eyebrow. There's not enough health benefits in the world to make kombucha palatable, but I keep that opinion to myself.

"Water's fine. Thank you, miss," I say with a nod. Her cheeks flush red and she spins around to grab a glass. She thinks I can't see that grin, but the dimple on the side of her cheek gives her away.

I chuckle to myself as my ego swells a bit. It's nice to know I still got it. The nice intern, or staff, or whatever she is, hands me the glass with a timid smile before she scampers off.

I sip and wait, sip and wait. Fifteen minutes later, Elle glides into the room in a short, flowy dress. It's a shade of deep brown, the same color as her doe eyes. Her light blond hair lies in loose waves over her shoulders. The nipped waist of the dress shows off her slim, shapely figure. Her legs look about five miles long.

She's beautiful, of course. That's part of the job in this town. But there's an intense, searching look in her eyes that makes me curious about her. She's vigilant, maybe apprehensive.

When she saunters over to the table and sits without introducing herself, or even shaking my hand, I bite back a twinge of annoyance. Where are this girl's manners?

"Good morning," I say, more like a question than a statement. I'm surprised I have to start the conversation, given that I'm at her dining table.

Whatever. Just get this sorted and get out of here.

"Morning. Do you want—oh, okay good," she says as I bring the glass to my lips. I pray the cool water will quell the strange flame growing in my belly. It's not like me to get flustered this way.

"You mind?" She asks as she gets up. Before I have a chance to answer, she scurries over to the fridge and pulls a bottle of kombucha before returning to her seat across from me. Her nose crinkles as she takes a long gulp.

"So," I say as I open her file on the table between us, "it looks like your main concern is the stalker, Cal Paterni. That still the case?"

She rubs her eye, then looks at the shimmering nude makeup on her fingertips and sighs. "Yeah...he comes around less, now. Only when he's drunk and coked out. Which, now that I say it, is most of the time," she looks sideways out the window with a distant expression. It's clear she's still worried.

"Alright. You'll continue to have 24 hour protection. I'll be seeing you during the day, then another one of my guys will cover 7 PM to 7 AM." Her eyes widen at my words.

"You'll be here every day?" She swallows hard as she waits for my response.

"Yup, you and me. I can assure you won't run into the issues you had with Richard," I say, knowing full well the only issue was his professional disinterest in the beautiful young actress he's assigned to protect.

He wouldn't stand up to her. I, on the other hand, won't hold back. She's going to learn some discipline under my watch, I'm sure of that.

"We need to lay down some ground rules," I tell her as I interlace my fingers on the table. She frowns at that.

"What kind of rules?" she asks apprehensively.

"Safety rules. First, your curfew is now 9 PM. No clubs without discussing with me first. That way I can get a few guys there before you arrive."

She balks at that. "I...," she starts, then trails off. Fire blooms in her eyes and she stares into mine defiantly.

"You're not the boss of me! I pay *you!*" she huffs. *Seems like the start of a tantrum*, I think to myself. I brace myself for her outburst, using my stern, calm voice.

Why lie? It's my Daddy voice. This little brat is drawing it out of me.

"Yes, you pay me. To keep you safe. So where that's concerned, I'm the boss of you," I tell her firmly.

A sea of emotions wash over her face — shock, confusion, irritation, concern. She's clearly skeptical of me but she sees my point regardless.

There's something else happening, too. The way she squirms in her chair as a flush creeps up her neck. Her shallow breath. Those big, warm eyes scanning me with a mixture of nerves and desire.

Yeah, I know that look.

She nods in agreement, then asks what the other rules are. I say keep curfew and to let me know if she has any concerns. She grumbles a bit before she agrees.

Times like this make me want to drop the whole project. Cash out my tech portfolio and run far away from the lovely, vulnerable woman who's woken up the butterflies in my stomach. Take my 900 million and fuck off to the woods, hand the keys to Richard, and never look back.

Too bad one look at Elle filled me with a bone deep need to protect her. And instead of running away, I'm going to see her all day, every day.

What could go wrong?

CHAPTER THREE

Leroy. More like LeRoyal Pain in my Ass. What an unbeliev-able, bossy jerk. I need him to protect me while I do what I want, not tell me what to do!

Our conversation makes me realize that no one has ever been firm with me. I was raised by nannies and cooks and house-keepers while my parents worked and partied. They let me run wild because my parents left no guidance about rules or discip-line and they needed to keep their jobs.

So here I am, still wild and needy and impulsive as a little kid. Big surprise.

I can't believe he spoke to me like that. After our brief con-versation, he walked through the house and around the grounds, looking for who knows what. I was grateful for a moment away from him to get my bearings back.

Why did it make me feel…good? Like I was contained, but not trapped. Accountable for my actions.

And wet. What the fuck is that about? My heart thumps in my chest and the pulse between my legs grows more intense.

After his rounds, Leroy pulls up a chair by the front door and reads. A real, paper book. For some reason, that's incredibly sexy to me.

I can't ignore his presence. My hairs are standing on end as my team does my makeup and curls my hair. I'm getting dolled up for a new round of Instagram posts.

Today, we're promoting mineral make-up, designer bathing suits, and impossible beauty standards. I can't help but wonder about how he sees me. I look at my life through his eyes and I see that it's utterly trivial.

They can keep the online clout and press attention. What I want more than anything is some intimate, special attention. To have someone see me clearly and know me deeply and love me no matter what. It's a lifelong thirst that no amount of money or likes can ever satisfy.

Leroy combs his hair away from his eyes as he reads. His hair is closely cropped on the sides, dark brown heavily salted with gray. It's a few inches longer on top, silky and poker straight. His short beard is salt-and-pepper gray on his strong, square jaw. Thick, sculpted muscle dances on his arms as he flips to the next page.

Clarence, my photographer, guides me into the spot they've lit and arranged for the shoot. He praises me as I pose, giving me cues about my expression and angles.

Self-conscious, I sneak a glance at Leroy. He's entranced by whatever he's reading, hardly bothered by the chattering team buzzing around me. He's bent over, resting those huge arms on his knees. His back is broad and meaty — so much so that I actually salivate a little.

"Yes, honey! That's the look, Elle. Give me more. Give me that pure lust!" Clarence chirps at me excitedly. Leroy casts me a sideways glance, ticking his eyebrow up. The moment our eyes meet, my stomach flips and my heart races. Damn this surly, bossy jerk. With his huge, gorgeous body and ruggedly handsome face.

After the shoot, I do hour after hour of paid video chat calls with fans. The money is going toward domestic violence education and prevention in California. Maybe some day I'll have my own foundation to help all the women like me who couldn't afford to escape the way I did. A chill passes over me at the thought.

Melinda serves marinated chicken, sweet potatoes, and roasted vegetables for dinner. She's a wizard at turning healthy meals into something absolutely seductive and delicious. The majority of staff trickle out by 5 PM and I sit alone on the deck, sipping a glass of dry red wine.

Uneasiness roils in my belly but I can't pinpoint why. The wine warms my insides as the setting sun warms my skin.

Like a lover, I think bitterly. Not that I'd know much about that. Cal was selfish and sporadic with his physical affection. He cheated openly and made sure to let me know it was my fault he was straying.

Fucking prick. I swallow the last of my wine and head inside. It's empty and quiet again. Leroy opens the front door and another man follows behind him. They're talking in low voices and I realize it's already 7 at night.

Leroy strides into the kitchen with the other man behind him. They're both enormous, but Leroy is tall as well as muscular. The other man, Bradley, is built like a keg and gives me a respectful nod when Leroy introduces him.

"Nine PM curfew. Got that?" He asks sternly, looking down at me with a serious intensity in his eyes. I cross my arms and grumble in agreement.

"Good. See you tomorrow," he says brusquely before seeing himself out. Bradley takes up his post by the entrance, pulling out his phone and scrolling endlessly.

I tell him that I'm going to bed and he wishes me goodnight. Once I shut the bedroom door, I feel a surge of energy.

I want to party. I need to. It's been so long and I'm aching for it.

Probably just want an escape.

No, that's not quite right. I want to be touched. Touched hungrily and greedily instead of being primped and prodded.

And maybe, just for a moment, I can get a break from this gnawing misery in my gut.

I throw on a fitted black dress and slip my black pumps into my bag. When I get confirmation that my ride is nearby, I slip out my window onto the lawn. The tiny patch of green is nearly impossible to keep alive, but today I'm thankful that I'm not walking over rocks and brush in my bare feet.

The driver waits at the end of my driveway, out of Bradley's sight. The older, heavyset woman tells me that I look beautiful. I nearly ask her if she's looking for a daughter, but instead stare out the window until we pull up to the club. She tries to hand the bill back, but I insist she take my $100 tip. I thank her again and head toward the bouncer.

He leads me through the back entrance of the club to the VIP area. I'm reminded of Cal sneaking me into clubs when I was still underage and how overwhelmed I was by the indulgent scene.

The lights are dim neon, orange and blue. It gives the crowded room a surreal, dreamy look. There's a small dance floor and many booths stuffed with beautiful people in expensive clothes. Cash, liquor, pills and powders are flowing freely. In the corner, I'm fairly certain a woman is getting fingered by her partner, pinned against the wall. I watch for a moment, concerned, until I see her smile and kiss him.

Lucky. I make my way around the room slowly, listening for sales pitches on designer drugs. I listen briefly before taking one from the man. When I offer him money, he turns me away.

"It's on the house," he says with a smile that makes me uneasy.

I can't tell you why I took it, exactly. It has a subtle bitter taste as it dissolves on my tongue. Before it comes on, I order a flute of champagne and take a seat at the bar.

The drink bubbles jubilantly on my tongue. I taste every single one. When I search the room, I see every detail. Information floods my senses — the bass in the music thumps through me, as if it's emanating from inside me. Patterns undulate and dance over every surface. Everywhere I look, I'm in wonder of the intricate, interconnected beauty of the scene around me.

The bartender gives me a fresh champagne and I make my way to the floor. My body flows with the music, my skin no longer a barrier between myself and the world but a porous, breathing entity that connects me to the pumping energy in the room.

As the music peaks, I start to wobble. Suddenly I feel way drunker than I should be — woozy and disoriented. Darkness seeps into the edges of my vision as my lips tingle before the light fades completely.

A lurch sends me flying forward into something hard. My head is slow and swimmy, like my brain is submerged in mud. A steady rumbling sound surrounds me in the cramped space where I'm stuck.

When I try to move — which is difficult in itself right now — I find my arms and legs bound. There's a dank, earthy taste on the fabric gagging my mouth. No matter how hard I blink, my vision won't clear.

"You awake back there, my little starlet?"

The familiar voice makes my blood run cold. I'd know it anywhere.

Cal.

The situation hits me in waves. I'm drugged. I'm bound. I'm in Cal's car headed to god knows where.

This is it. This is the night that he makes good on his promises and scrubs me from the earth for good. Despite my fight to stay conscious, the leaden darkness washes over me again and I fade out.

CHAPTER FOUR

Leroy

Unbelievable. Absolutely fucking unbelievable.

Bradley called me at 1 AM to tell me that the girl was gone. Elle is a grown woman, sure, but she acts all of about fifteen. Breaking curfew on her very first night? That's a message.

She's calling out for someone to set boundaries. Someone to be consistent and keep her in line.

Tonight, that person is me.

My teeth gnash as I speed through the dark, winding streets. If she's hurt...

Nope. Not entertaining that. Because I'm going to find her.

The club security footage showed Cal carrying her out. Yes, I hacked their security system. But that's besides the point.

I pull up the tracking app and watch the blip turn and then eventually stop. Elle is obsessed with her privacy, and rightly so, but Cal was easy to track down. He broadcasts his every move on social media. Slipping a tracker under the wheel well of his car had been a breeze.

Richard texts that he's at the location — a complex of storage units sprawling in every direction. I skid into the gravel lot and Richard messages the unit number. I practically barrel out of my truck before putting it in park.

As I approach the unit I see Richard at the ready. Inside, there's frantic, incoherent screaming. It's Cal. I don't hear a peep from Elle. Fire roars through my body as I throw the unit door open, spilling cold fluorescent light into the dark room.

Cal whips around and stares at us with wild, glassy eyes. His face is deep red, nearly plum, from rage and screaming. He starts to yell before I lunge forward, tackling him to the ground.

That's when I see Elle. She's bound at the wrists and ankles and buckled in to a bucket racing seat, sitting lopsided on the floor. Her eyes are puffy and red from crying and she looks dazed.

Red floods my vision. I pummel the man beneath me with my huge fist. Disgusting piece of shit. I rain blows down on his twisted, hateful face. His screams turn to garbled moans before Richard pulls me off and drags Cal out of the unit.

"Get the girl," he hollers as he drags Cal by the ankles out toward the parking lot.

As if I needed reminding. It's a fucking ghastly sight. She stares at me with vacant, wide-eyed fear as I remove the gag, then cut the ties at her wrists and ankles.

"He's gone, hon. You're safe now," I tell her as I take her hand.

"Gone?" She looks up at me in wide-eyed confusion. Her voice is soft and quiet. Small.

God damn it. My heart wrenches at the sight of this beautiful woman so vulnerable and alone. Terrified. Unprotected.

Not anymore.

"I got you, Elle," I say as I scoop her up into my arms. She's limp as a rag doll and nearly as light. Poor little Ellie bird.

Ellie bird. Jesus, man. Get it together.

But I can't help but be affected by the delicate, lost girl in my arms. Her head bobs languidly against my chest as I approach the truck. Richard's got Cal tied and gagged on the ground with a boot on his back.

It's half what he deserves, but right now, he's not my concern.

"Deliver him to the station. Tell them what you saw," I call to Richard. He nods and yanks Cal to his feet and tosses him into the back of his truck. He'll have a fun ride bouncing around in that closed shell all the way back into the city.

I shimmy the passenger door open and lift Elle inside. "You're safe now," I tell her gently as I buckle her seatbelt.

The pained disbelief that contorts her face will stay with me forever. It tears at my fucking heart.

I drive back to her place and scoop her out of the truck. Bradley is waiting at the door with a new recruit, Dan. I'd sent him over when Bradley gave me the call.

"Place's clear, boss," Bradley tells me as he opens the door for me. Dan gawks for a minute at Elle in my arms but masks his surprise quickly.

"Gimme one more sweep," I say as I carry Elle toward her bedroom. He nods and they head in opposite directions around the perimeter.

I know that's probably irrational — Cal is in police custody now. But who knows what kind of garbage that piece of shit associated with, and if he shared information about Elle out of spite.

I won't take any chances with her. Not after tonight.

I lay her gently on the bed when Bradley knocks on the door frame. All quiet. I thank them and dismiss them for the evening.

"You sure, boss?" Bradley asks, unable to hide his surprise at my worried face, hunched at Elle's bedside. I shoot him a glance that answers his question. He nods and turns, ushering Dan out with him.

My eyes turn back to Elle. She's curled under the covers in some space between consciousness and shock. Who knows what she's got in her system?

A light bulb goes off in my mind. "Be right back, hon," I say quietly before hustling down to the kitchen. She's gotta have something...

My eyes dart around the refrigerator. Bingo. I pull out a bottled chocolate protein shake before snagging my first aid kid from the truck. When I get back to the bedroom, Elle's sitting up in bed.

She looks at the kit in one hand and the shake in the other. "... What happened?" she asks softly.

You snuck out and got kidnapped, I nearly reply. Instead, I kneel down beside her bed and ask what she remembers.

"The nice lady driver," she says, bringing her thumb and forefinger to the bridge of her nose in frustration. "I went to the club and took something, I think."

My jaw winds tight at her words. So reckless. And fucking dangerous. But this isn't the time for a lecture.

"Then you were there. On top of..." her hand flutters over her mouth with a gasp. Her breathing quickens and she starts to shake.

"You're safe now, Elle" I assure her. My hand hovers over her quaking leg before landing on her shin. I want to ground her, but she's just been through something traumatic. I don't want to scare her more with the wrong touch.

"Shh, easy girl. Deep breaths," I coo, looking up at her. She trembles through a few ragged breaths before she gets a handle on it.

"Good girl," I whisper. Oops. To my surprise, tears well in her eyes and she reaches toward me, her hands opening and closing in unison.

Grabby hands. Fucking end me.

"C'mere," I say as I swing my arm open and edge my hips onto the bed beside her. She collapses into my side, breaking into hard, wrenching sobs.

"Let it out, hon," I cue as I rub my hand over her back. I can feel her ribs as I rub. She's too damn thin. Her arms wrap around my waist and hold me tight. When she's calm, I pull the shake off the bedside table.

"I'm not sure what's in your system," I say as I twist the cap open, "but you could use the nutrients."

She furrows her brow and fumbles for the bottle. "Uh uh," I say as I draw it away. "Let me."

I bring the bottle to her lips and the look she gives me shreds me inside.

It's longing. Earnest, pure longing. And adoration.

Fuck. This sweet little girl is destroying my resolve.

I hold her close as she drinks it down. When she's finished, I set the bottle aside and wrap my arms around her. We melt there for a long moment. Neither one of us wants to move, but I know that I should. I can't be falling in love with his needy, rebellious little brat.

Wish my damn heart would listen to me.

Her lids start to droop and I stir her. "One more thing, Elle," I whisper. She likely won't enjoy this next part.

"You need to go potty?" I ask casually, as if it's something I'd ask anyone in passing.

"No!" she whines, jutting her lower lip out at me.

"I think you do, honey. And I need to know what you've taken tonight." I retrieve the small plastic cup from the first aid kid and show it to her.

She blinks a couple of times, frowning at the cup. She must still be out of it.

"Am I in trouble?" she asks me in a tiny voice. Whether it's little space, drugs, shock, or a combination of all three, I don't know.

Okay, Leroy. Time to put your Daddy skills to the test.

"No, baby, not at all," I assure her as I take her hand. "I need to know so that I can take care of you."

She stares at me like I'm speaking Latin. Then she sucks her bottom lip into her mouth and nods in agreement.

"That's my good girl. Here we go," I murmur as I draw her up into my arms.

Not your good girl, I chide myself. When I feel nuzzle into my chest, every cell in my body wishes that she was.

I set her down on the toilet and rest my hands on her ankles.

"I'm going to take your panties off now, hon. No funny business."

I have to shimmy her tight dress up over her hips before I can get her underwear off. It's a sheer black thong, hardly larger than a postage stamp with dental floss straps.

"Daddy, please," she murmurs, staring at me dreamily. She presses her thighs together and whimpers softly.

Not yours. Not yours. It's the drugs talking, that's it.

"It's okay, baby. Nothing I haven't seen before." I pat her on the leg and rise to stand. When I don't leave the room, she crosses her arms over her chest.

"Can't go wif you here!" she huffs. Of course she can't.

"I know, baby girl. But I have to hold the cup. And I can't risk you toppling over and cracking your head open," I say, more firmly.

I spin to turn on the tap, hoping that will encourage her. I kneel in front of her and position the cup, then look away. Her pubic hair is trimmed into a cute, neat V above her gorgeous little cunt. I couldn't help but notice.

After a moment she grunts in frustration. "I can't!" she cries from behind me. The tap is on full blast and my frazzled brain spins trying to churn up solutions.

Fuck. She's exhausted, high and traumatized and this is the last stop between her and her bed. Gotta get this over with.

"If it keeps on rainin', the levee's going to break," I sing quietly. What the fuck am I doing? It was the last song I'd heard in the car on my way home, before I got that late night call from Bradley.

I repeat the line, my voice reverberating off all the tile in the bathroom. By the second verse, I hear liquid hit the cup. Success!

"Full," she blurts out and I instinctively draw the cup away. I set it on the counter and help her over to the sink. I stand behind her to steady her and lather her hands up under the warm water. They're so soft and delicate in mine.

"You did a good job, baby. I know that wasn't easy. Thank you, sweetheart. Such a good girl." I see a small smile cross her lips in her reflection. It's fucking beautiful.

By the time I'm done drying our hands, the test is complete. She's positive for MDMA, roofies, and marijuana, though that's likely not from tonight. The good news is that everything will run it's course. Just need to keep her hydrated, then fed.

Precious little thing. I carry her back to bed and tuck the sheets under her chin. There's a loveseat between the bed and the wall-to-wall closet where I flop down and try to relax. Her re- laxed, sleepy breathing hits me like the sweetest music and I drift off.

CHAPTER FIVE

Leroy was constantly on my mind after that day. When I woke up in a panic the next morning, the first thing I saw was Leroy's huge body curled up on the couch, asleep. He'd stayed all night, which made my heart swell.

He tells me that the police report Richard filed was enough to warrant a permanent restraining order on Cal. Between the kidnapping charge and his admission that he'd bribed the bartender to drug me, the case is rock solid. It takes a while to process, but Leroy assured me that if he ever shows up again, he'll go to jail. "And that's only if he doesn't run into me first," he growled.

The memory sends a shiver down my spine. He's so protective. So stern. There's a sexual attraction, no doubt, but something deeper than lust draws me toward him. A longing for intense, lasting love.

I don't want to admit it, but after that night, I turned myself over to him. I didn't tell him so but I did start following his rules. It actually makes the days easier to have some structure and to know that someone is keeping an eye on me.

Leroy stayed reserved and professional after my rescue. Neither of us brought up what happened between us, but it's palpable in the air when we're near each other.

It's been eight weeks since the kidnapping. I double-check my appearance in the mirror before I head into kitchen. Today I'm wearing pale pink thigh highs, a black skater skirt, and a matching pale pink peasant top. Cute as hell, if I say so myself.

I love the mornings more than ever now. Between 7 and 9, it's just he and I. I step onto the deck and soak in the sunshine with one ear listening for his truck crunching down the driveway.

A few moments later, that thrilling sound starts to creep closer. I head inside and meet him in the foyer.

"Good morning, Elle," he says with a smile. He gets a dimple in his right cheek when he smiles that drives me absolutely wild. I say good morning and wave him into the kitchen behind me.

"I have good news today," he calls to me. I bound over to the coffee pot and fill two mugs. We sit across from each other at the dining table and my body hums with anticipation.

"What is it?" I try to ask casually, but my voice breaks at the end. *Smooth, Elle.*

"We just got word that the restraining order is approved and active. Cal will never bother you again," he declares. Relief washes over me and I let out a heavy sigh. Good fucking riddance.

Leroy takes in my expression as he raises the mug to his lips. Those full, gorgeous lips framed by his salt and pepper beard. I squeeze my thighs together to quiet the throb between them.

"Guess you don't need me anymore, huh?" he asks after a beat. There's a twinge of sadness in his voice. The words rattle me as panic rises in my throat.

No. God, no. Don't leave. He can't leave. I stare at him pleadingly, unable to conjure any words through my dry, tight throat.

This is it. It's now or never.

I reach across the table and take his hands in mine. He startles in surprise and watches me carefully as I draw in a deep, shaky breath.

"I do need you. More than you know." I squeeze his huge, rough hands tight in mine. I confess that I'd never felt more loved than the night he stayed and tended to me. Nobody ever cared for me like that before. Tears burn in the corners of my eyes and I try to blink them away.

"I'll keep paying, just, please, don't leave…" I trail off. The next words are barely a whisper.

"Could even pay you to be my Daddy…" I offer, embarrassed at my desperation. When he rises to stand, I'm sure that this is the end and he's heading for the door.

What he does instead shocks me. He approaches me and helps me stand, then pulls me into his arms. My whole body lights up in response to his touch. I've been starving to be close to him ever since that night.

"I don't want to leave you, Elle," he murmurs into my hair. A large hand brushes a strand from my face and runs down the back of my neck. He swallows hard before continuing.

"You've been on my mind ever since I found you with that cruel bastard. A sweet girl in desperate need of guidance and protection. Deep in my heart, I knew I wanted to be that protector." He lets out a sigh and pulls back slightly, holding me by the shoulders.

"If we go down this road, that feeling's only going to get stronger. And I'm going to expect more from you than the average Joe. I'm a Daddy Dom, and I need to care for my partner like my precious little girl. To dote on her when he's good and discipline her over my knee when she acts up." His searing stare bores into me, his dark eyes gleaming with conviction.

"I could tell," I admit, using all my might to hold his intense gaze. "Pieces of that night came back to me over time. I remember what happened…and that you met my little," I eke out.

Those mysterious, dark eyes track me as I muster the next words.

"...Do you believe in fate, Leroy?"

He scoffs, his hands trailing from my shoulders down my arms to hold my hands in his.

"No, not exactly," he says, shaking his head with a smirk. He steps closer to close the gap between us. "But pretty flowers grow from shit, right?"

What the fuck kind of blue collar aphorism is that? The image of a daisy rising triumphantly from a turd makes me crack up. Nerves crank my laughter into overdrive until a tear rolls down my cheek.

Yes, bad things can lead to good things. But the visual is sending me.

"Alright," he chuckles, arching an eyebrow at my cackling. A swipe of his thumb brushes the stray tear from my face.

The warmth in his gaze hits me in my core. The words bubble up from deep within me.

"If this is the road that led me to you, I wouldn't change a single step," I murmur, leaning my head against his chest.

Hah, how's he like that? He's not the only one who can come up with a fitting metaphor.

Leroy lets out a low chuckle and squeezes me tight. Excitement churns wildly inside me like a hurricane rising from the sea.

Fuck it. I arch up and plant my lips on his. He's tentative at first, then opens up to my curious lips. Our tongues meet and he devours me.

His kiss is ravenous. Powerful.

Dominant.

It sweeps everything else away. I melt into him as every cell in my body cries out for his touch.

"Please, play with me, Daddy," I beg in his ear. His body braces in response to my words. I look up, pleading, drunk on the knowledge that I'm having an effect on him.

"Bedroom, girl. Now." His firm tone makes my whole body shudder with anxious excitement.

I try to scamper off but his hand anchors me. When we cross into the bedroom, I spin to face him and he picks me up, carrying me over to the wall of windows and pressing my back firmly against the glass. I wrap my arms and legs around him and moan into our kiss.

He's so fucking strong. Being handled like a plaything has my panties soaking wet. My skirt is bunched up around my hips so there's only my panties between me and the hard bulge in his denim jeans.

The kiss leaves me breathless and swirling with lust. It's like everything before him has fallen away, burned up by the intensity of our desire for one another.

"Fucking gorgeous, Elle," he growls as he sucks at the flesh of my neck. Everywhere our skin meets evokes a rush of electric heat that makes my clit throb.

"Please, please," I beg, my body pulsing with need. He sets me down gently on my feet, then kneels down to tug my panties off.

Instead of rising back up, he latches onto my mound with his mouth, making me scream with shock and delight. Holy fucking shit.

His tongue works between my labia and over my aching clit in tight, lapping circles. My legs shake beneath me and I brace myself against the window for balance. I clutch my skirt tight in my fists, keeping it out of the way as Leroy looks up at me, that wicked tongue ripping every ounce of pleasure from my body.

The sun warms my back and I have a fleeting thought about the paparazzi catching shots of my bare ass pressed against the glass. Let them see. I'm not afraid anymore. Not now that Leroy's here.

He grunts with satisfaction as he drinks me in, feasting on me greedily. When he digs two thick fingers inside and curls them against my sweet spot, I cry out like an animal. Each precise touch draws my climax nearer. I'm panting and trembling as the hot pressure builds in my core.

"That's it, baby girl. Come for me. Come for Daddy," he growls.

My body obeys in spades. The pleasure bubbles up and then breaks me open, hitting me with wave after wave of warm, electric ecstasy. He works me through my orgasm until I'm limp, then picks me up and carries me to bed.

"My good girl," he rumbles in my ear. "Fucking perfect." He peels my top off and kisses down my chest. I cry out as his rough hands knead my breasts. "All mine."

My heart soars from his possessive praise. With Leroy, I feel more desired than ever. It's not just sexual — he wants me, with all my struggles and my attitude. Even my needy little side.

I'm on my back with my legs in the air, my hips at the edge of the bed. I'm wide open, but desire has burned away any shred of shame. Leroy eyes me hungrily as he trails a finger over my slippery slit before stripping off his shirt and pants.

Jiminy Christmas. His body is unreal. Burly and broad, bound with chiseled muscle. Salt and pepper hair dusts his chest and lower stomach, leading my eyes down to the thick, hard cock bouncing free from his underwear. My mouth hangs open at the tremendous sight.

Leroy's eyes are pure fire. *Wow.* It's intoxicating to be the subject of his lust. He lowers himself onto me so that the warm, smooth head of his cock teases against my entrance.

"Please, Daddy," I whimper, struggling to work myself down onto him. He keeps me at bay, clearly pleased at the sight of my desperation for him.

"Tell me," he growls.

"F-fuck me, Daddy, please," I whisper in his ear, my skin ablaze at the sound of my own naughty words.

He enters me slowly, watching my face as each inch of him stretches me open with a sweet, decadent sting. He's touching parts of me no man has ever reached — physically or emotionally. It's as if this is my first time all over again.

Leroy growls with pleasure when he's inside me to the hilt. "So good, baby. So tight around Daddy's cock," he thunders in my ear as he grabs my hips firmly, fucking me with deep, deliberate strokes.

Ugh, his words. Those low grunts of bestial pleasure. The sight of him above me, looming so large that his shadow swallows me up. I'm nearing the edge again, reveling in Leroy's dominance. I'm completely his, at long last.

I wail and writhe under his pounding thrusts. He fucks me harder, growling with exertion and enjoyment with each rough pump. When he reaches between my legs to rub my clit, the sensation hits me so hard I swear I see stars.

"Fuck yes, baby. Come with me," he roars, spurring my orgasm. My pleasure crests as he bucks into me erratically, gasping and moaning as he fills me with his satisfaction.

We lay entwined until he softens, then he lays down beside me on the bed, pulling me close so that my head rests on his chest, our arms around one another.

We talk for a long time in the warm cocoon of blankets. How our first time went, what we'd like to try, our limits, some basic rules. It's easy to be open and honest with someone who accepts you, I just learned.

"Hope this doesn't effect business," I tease. He chuckles.

"Daddy Dom isn't a service I offer to anyone else," he murmurs into my hair, then punctuates it with a kiss. His body stiffens and I hear him sigh.

"What is it?" I ask.

"Well, I have a confession," he says, brushing his hair back from his forehead with his free hand.

Oh god. Of course it was too good to be true. He's married. He's moving to Thailand. He's a spy.

"I, uh, don't exactly need to work. At all." I crane up to look at him, waiting for him to continue.

"What are you telling me?" I prompt after a pause.

He explains that he has investments worth nearly a billion dollars. Inherited some money from his no-good father and invested it nearly a decade ago. Since, it's grown to a substantial fortune.

I'm sure the surprise is carved into my face. My mind reels — this means he could be my full time Daddy. We could go anywhere in the world and build a life together. Would he want that?

"I know what I feel for you, Elle," he tells me, as if he read my mind. "We can play however you want. Take things slow. The future is whatever we want to make it," he says, rubbing his warm hand over my upper back.

"I want you. I want more," I say, the last word stretching out with a long yawn.

"I want a nap," I joke, wiping the sleepy mist from my eyes.

Leroy chuckles at that. "Seems like a good place to start," he coos, turning on his side and holding me close. The warmth where our bodies meet melts into a pool that swallows me up in an easy, peaceful slumber.

EPILOGUE

Elle — Two Years Later

I was thrilled to step away from the spotlight. It's the only life I've ever known and I was desperate for change. With Leroy, I wanted to explore everything and eat up the whole world.

I've lived more in that single year than I had in the past 27.

Leroy handed company operations over to Richard, who's doing great. Business is growing and he's taken naturally to leadership. It was a big relief for him to let that go and dive headfirst into our new life.

We spent our first year together traveling. Ancient ruins in the Amazon. Old European cities with their gray clouds and pointy architecture. Enjoying the art, food, and natural wonders everywhere we went. But more than anything, we enjoyed each other.

No matter where we are, we can't keep our hands off of each other. There's a soul-level magnetism between us. The lust is a lot of fun, of course, but our loving bond is unbreakably strong. We're sustained by a bottomless well of adoration and gratitude for one another.

He's taken me everywhere. And I mean *taken* me. Screaming over the crystal blue open ocean as he fucks me over the rail of our private cabana. Soft and sensual riding in the Icelandic glacial hot springs. Making me come under my lap tray on our first class flight, smiling wickedly as I struggle to keep quiet.

That's become one of his favorites, the pervert. I couldn't possibly love him more.

We talk about getting married, but we're not in a rush. We know that we're meant for one another, and neither one of us is a big fan of listening to other people's rules. That gets me over Daddy's knee more often than I'd like to admit.

There's nowhere in the world I'd rather be.

When we grew wary of traveling, we started searching for a place to live. I know this is the worst thing to complain about, but we had so many options that it was hard to decide. Finally, we found a gorgeous, mid-century bungalow in New Zealand, near the coast. Leroy and I both missed being near the ocean.

Our life is quiet now — surfing, cooking lots of fish and fresh fruit, and simply enjoying one another. Leroy started a new security firm in Auckland. He said relaxation is sweeter when it's earned. If it makes him happy, I'm not going to argue. I admire his endless work ethic.

Not to be outdone, I finally started a foundation for survivors of domestic violence. The international organization grants relief funds to women in danger to escape their situations, as well as money for confidential shelters and community education. If I can keep just one woman from enduring what I went through, it'll be worth it.

There aren't enough words in the world to convey how grateful I am for my wonderful life with Leroy, my brave rescuer. My stern, loving, forever Daddy. He's given me more than I ever imagined for myself.

BOOKS BY THIS AUTHOR

Ranger Daddy

Environmental activism. A shrewd oil company. A surly forest ranger and a lookout tower.

These are the ingredients in the sh*t smoothie Ashley walks into at an anti-drilling protest. Feisty and idealistic, Ashley bites back against the gruff, dominant forest ranger. When violence erupts, she finds herself helpless in his strong arms. Alone in the ranger tower, Ashley and ranger Christopher struggle for power. How did he end up taking care of this wild little brat? And will she get her way and finally find the Daddy Dom she's been searching for? See how their steamy story unfolds in this quick instalove, daddy dom discipline erotica.

Daddy's Protection

A thief broke into her apartment. Then Roland broke into her heart.

Cam never stood a chance at resisting him. Not with those huge, rippling muscles covered in tattoos. Those dark, searching eyes. He's the hero she least expected, but needed more than anything. There's an effortless chemistry between Cam and Roland that makes her wonder. Could he be the Daddy Dom she's always longed for? Or will he reject her, like the others before, when she shares her little side? Look inside this steamy, instalove, age play romance to find out!

Fated

Wendy is at the end of her rope. She's lost everything because of who she is: a little. No job, no family, nothing to keep her off of the roof of her twenty story apartment building. Except Shawn.

The gruff, rugged veteran has faced indescribable darkness himself. He sees Wendy's pain. He won't let her face her problems without backup. She can't help but fall for the way this huge, dominant man dotes on her tenderly. Heartfelt, raw, and steamy —this hot BDSM romance between an ABDL baby girl and her loving Daddy Dom will have you begging for more!

Content note: This story contains discussion of suicidality and suicidal ideation.

Daddy's Debt

Candace and Liam would never have met if her father wasn't a selfish, thieving monster. She's on the hook for his newest debt and muscle-bound Liam has been sent to collect. Candace's openhearted, innocent spirit unlocks Liam's desire to protect. To nurture. To dominate. For all the things her father has taken from her in her life, Candace never expected his mistakes to lead her to the type of man she's only dreamed of — her caring, protective Daddy Dom.

Saved By The Champion

Mitchell, better known as "Twisted Mitch," is a professional wrestler famous for his agility and enormous size. He's the last person Lisa expected to emerge from the dark of night to rescue her. She didn't expect anyone to help her. She's at rock bottom: scorned by her family, all alone in the world after an ex reveals her deepest secret. Under Mitchell's discipline, Lisa learns how to love herself for the first time. Through her submission to her doting Daddy Dom, Lisa tastes the security and freedom she's always longed for.

CLAIM YOUR FREE STORY!

Ani has made a terrible mistake. After breaking one of her longest standing rules with her Daddy, Brady, she confesses everything. Brady is tender and comforting, but stern when it comes to punishment. Join this established, loving DDlg couple for some steamy discipline over Daddy's knee!

Sign up for my newsletter to receive your FREE copy of Ani's Confession! Exclusively for new subscribers!!

THANK YOU FOR READING

Thank you so much for supporting my work. I love writing about this lifestyle and you make it possible!

Want a FREE eBook? Sign up for my newsletter to receive an exclusive story!! Plus sneak-peaks and snippets of my upcoming work! No spam, ever — pinkie swear.

Follow me on Amazon Author Central to stay up to date on my publications!

'Til next time,
Sonia